Mystery of the Mixed-Up Teacher

The Dallas O'Neil Mysteries

MYSTERY OF THE MIXED-UP TEACHER

by

JERRY B. JENKINS

MOODY PRESS
CHICAGO

ISBN: 0-8024-8377-1

1 2 3 4 5 6 Printing/ LC /Year 92 91 90 89 88

Printed in the United States of America

To Clair Miller,
tireless and selfless

Contents

1

The Game

That's what Jimmy Calabresi and I thought it was—a game. We figured that Mrs. Lucas decided we could have some fun with just a month to go in sixth grade. All we thought about all day was baseball anyway, he and I and the other Baker Street Sports Club members in her class. And she knew it.

She had always made studying fun. She was the best teacher we'd ever had. It was nice to have a teacher who went to the same church I did. I had known her and her husband and family for as long as I could remember. In fact, she and her husband and one of her two grown sons had each been my Sunday school teacher at one time or another.

That's why, when she did something strange, we thought she was kidding.

School ended at three thirty everyday, and Jimmy and I could be home on our bikes by five to four. We'd meet the rest of the guys and be on the ball diamond no later than four fifteen. That gave us an hour and a half before we had to start heading home to dinner.

The key to getting home by five to four, though, was that Mrs. Lucas always gave the signal that we could leave, usually before the bell stopped ringing. She was a stickler about that.

She didn't like kids to start getting their stuff together too early. At three twenty-nine she would look at the clock, then smile at us and give a small nod.

That meant we could take the next minute to put our stuff away, stack the things we wanted to take home, and sit still, waiting for the bell. If anyone was moving while the bell was ringing, Mrs. Lucas just sat there, waiting.

When everyone was perfectly still, she would give us another nod, and we could leave—no running till we got outside. With a month to go, she crossed us up. At least, that's how it seemed. At three twenty-nine, she was sitting at her desk, gazing at us as we read an assignment.

No one noticed that she hadn't looked at the clock or nodded. We just did what we had done everyday for the last eight months and started getting our things together. At first I thought she might stop us and remind us that she had not given us the signal yet, but then I thought maybe I had just missed it.

We were all busily getting ready, and she was still sitting there. I thought we were quiet when the bell rang, but as we watched her, nothing happened. The bell stopped ringing, and she hadn't nodded yet. Worse, she didn't seem to even be looking at us. She was just staring, but not at anyone in particular.

This was so new to me that I didn't know what to think. From my desk in the front row, I swung around and shot a quick glance at everyone else in the room. I sure thought someone must be moving or talking or not ready. There was no other reason for Mrs. Lucas to hold us there.

No one else even returned my gaze. Everyone's eyes were riveted to Mrs. Lucas—even Jimmy's. Usually we would trade a knowing look when something funny or unusual happened. We had even got into trouble for that a few times. But now he just stared at her, his face quizzical.

A minute passed. I half expected Mrs. Lucas to scold me for having whirled around in my seat, but it was as if she hadn't noticed. I finally decided that she was just daydreaming, thinking about something else, or upset about something. It was clear she hadn't heard the bell.

I raised my hand. She didn't notice. I waved it, which she doesn't like. She didn't notice. I kept my hand up and spoke softly. "Mrs. Lucas?"

In slow motion she turned and looked at me. Then she smiled. "Good morning, Dallas," she said. "Yes, what is it?"

"It's the bell, ma'am."

"The bell?"

Now I knew she was kidding. I laughed. "Yes! The bell!"

"Well, then," she said, rising. "I guess we'd better get started." She moved toward her desk and her lesson plans, which she had already covered that day.

Everyone was silent until someone started to giggle. This had to be a joke. Soon we were all laughing.

Mrs. Lucas looked up suddenly. "What time is it?" she asked, not unkindly.

"It's after three thirty," Jimmy said, his dark eyes still clouded with questions. "Can we go?"

"What are you all still doing here?" Mrs. Lucas said. "You'd better run along home. Does anyone need help with his wrap?"

We looked at each other and bolted for the door. She hadn't nodded, but clearly she had told us to run along. *Run along?* I hadn't heard that since I was a little kid.

Jimmy caught up with me, just as I was slamming my locker. "Did you hear what she said?" he asked, shaking his head so his shock of black hair bounced.

"Yeah, she said we should run along."

"No, Dal! I mean about helping us with our wraps? Just like in kindergarten or first grade! And anyway, who wears a wrap—whatever that is—in May?"

I shrugged. "You think this is one of her riddles? A game? Something we were supposed to notice?"

"That's what I was wondering. Like that time she left the class three different times during the day and came back with a different outfit on each time. I didn't notice until she told us."

"Me either, but remember that one of those times was after lunch, and she didn't change all that much."

"That was when we were studying crime detection and prevention," Jimmy said. "It was a pretty good little game she played. We really watched her from then on."

"Good pun. I remember."

Jimmy and I were on our bikes by now. He looked at me. "What are you talking about, Dallas?"

"You didn't have to say you watched her to remind me that you noticed the next day when all of a sudden she wasn't wearing her watch."

"I had forgotten that!" Jimmy insisted.

"Sure you did," I said, teasing him. He probably *had* forgotten it, but I wouldn't have. Mrs. Lucas was pretty impressed. He was the first, and as far as we knew, the only kid in the class who had noticed.

"Hey," he had said, "what happened to your watch?"

"Very observant, James!" she had said. "Did you just notice? I took it off during recess and haven't worn it for more than an hour."

She was teaching us to notice details the way detectives do. Learning all that stuff about police work was the most fun I had ever had in school. And that was saying something, because Mrs. Lucas always made things fun and interesting.

Once when we were studying electricity, she put two pieces of metal in a lemon and had us touch our tongues to the metal. We felt a very small static electric charge, not enough to even make us jump. She was showing us that lots of things carry electric charges that we would never expect. I'll never forget it.

Another time, she took the whole class to the place where a little girl had been run over by a car and killed. It had happened near another school, and a student crossing guard had been there. Mrs. Lucas explained how it had happened, how the guard had insisted that everyone wait, and how the little girl had darted into the street.

We spent a lot of time talking about the school board's changing to all adult crossing guards right after that and how that must have made the student guard feel. We decided as a class that he probably felt it was his fault, but Mrs. Lucas told us that the board had told him they knew he had done everything he could. The board just thought that children might obey an adult better.

I even remembered the time Mrs. Lucas explained how the city water system worked. We wondered why pressure didn't build up in the faucets when the taps weren't open, and she had a city water worker come in and explain it.

Mrs. Lucas was one great teacher. We toured the local newspaper, a bakery, and even a soup canning plant. I learned a lot, and it didn't even seem like school.

That's why, by the time Jimmy and I had dumped our books at our houses and changed clothes and got to the ball field, I was still wondering what Mrs. Lucas had been up to. No one else had arrived yet, so Jimmy and I were just warming up, lazily tossing the ball back and forth as we slowly backed away from each other.

"I just remembered something else," Jimmy said. "She said good morning to you."

"I know. You think it's a clue?"

"Has to be. But to what?"

"This is some sort of a quiz or something," I said. "If she does anything at all like this tomorrow, I'm gonna start taking notes."

"Good idea," Jimmy said. "Then as soon as we figure it out, we spring the solution on her. She'll be impressed, don't you think?"

I nodded, but I was beginning to dream of another way to impress her. "You know, Jim," I said, "we need to start thinking about a gift for her or a party or something."

"You mean the whole class?"

I nodded. "I've never had a teacher like her. Have you?"

"No, and I don't guess I ever will again, either."

"Then we should do something for her. Something nice."

"You mean something more than everybody surprising her with a message written on the board when she comes in the last day of school?"

"Course. That doesn't surprise anybody anymore. Every class does that. In fact, last year, Mr. Knuth purposely came in late that last day so we'd be sure to have enough time to get all the messages written."

"Yeah, and then he acted surprised that all the maps and the movie screen were pulled down over the board. He goes over to them and says, 'Hey, what are all these doing down?' pretending to be mad. 'I'd better pull these up so we can get started with class.' "

I laughed at the memory. "And he pulled them all up, pretending not to notice anything on the board. Finally, Jack Bastable points up there and says, 'Hey, Mr. Knuth! Look what we did!' "

"He was a pretty good teacher."

"You bet. But nothing like Mrs. Lucas."

"Did I hear you guys say my name?" It was big Jack Bastable, already over six feet tall, but our age. He leaned his bike up against the backstop and loped over.

Jimmy tossed the ball to him. "Yup, you did," Jimmy said. "But we weren't laughing at you."

2

Advice

J ack Bastable was not the violent type, and it was a good
thing. He was mentally retarded, and kids did make fun of
him sometimes. Not his friends, of course. Like Jimmy, we always made sure Jack knew we were not laughing at him.

A lot of people don't realize that most mentally retarded
people know they are mentally retarded. Jack sure did. He had
a great family. His parents encouraged him and his two sisters—who were normal—to try anything and everything in life.

We were so glad when the Bastables moved into our area.
We had met Jack when our Baker Street Sports Club basketball
team played against his. He was so much bigger than the rest
of us that the rumor got around that he was seven feet tall. Of
course, we all believed it.

Then, because even though he's our age he talks sort of
like someone who is about five, he didn't say anything at all
during a game. That made him seem scary. We watched some
early games, just to see what he was like, and a couple of times,
when he went up for a rebound or came down with one, some
smaller guys would bounce off him and hit the floor.

No one was seriously hurt, but if you have it in your mind
that this guy is about twenty-five years old, quiet, and mean,

you can convince yourself of anything. We allowed ourselves to be convinced that he was one mean guy who had lied about his age to get into the league.

He played so well on both offense and defense—and his retardation had no effect on his coordination—that we had no clue to the fact that he was different. When we found out, well, it changed our whole attitude about him. Then he moved near us and joined our club, and the more we got to know him, the nicer a guy we knew he was.

It seemed only right that his handicap should be balanced by his gift for athletics. He was well-proportioned, a great soccer goalie, a fast runner, could throw hard and fast and far, was a good fielder—especially at first base—and was a power hitter.

"What were you boys laughing about?" he asked, as we included him in our game of catch. We told him. He had started in a special school that year, but he remembered Mrs. Lucas and most of the kids in our class.

"Mrs. Lucas is a funny lady," he said. And he threw back his head and laughed with such glee that we had to laugh with him.

Within a few minutes, the rest of the guys were there, and we tried to play a practice game and talk at the same time. Which never works.

During the game Andy and Toby and Ryan—our smallest member—jogged in from the outfield while I was pitching.

"Hey!" I said. "That's only two outs!"

"We know," Andy said. "We just want to protest."

"Protest what? This is a practice game against our own teammates. What's to protest?"

"Well, we'd sign a petition, if that would help," Andy said. "We just want you and Jimmy to quit asking everybody's advice about your teacher and get on with the game. You've already figured out that she's got some sort of a quiz or riddle going on, so let's play ball, huh?"

I couldn't argue with that. Usually *I* had to get the guys' minds back on the game. Now *they* were doing it to *me*. And just in time. Jack was coming to bat. I could usually get him out, because he wasn't a refined hitter. When he got hold of the ball, it would go, and in practice it was more important for me to let him hit than to try to strike him out all the time. It didn't make any sense to discourage your power hitter.

I always coached him as I pitched. "Now, Jack," I would holler as he dug in, "don't swing for the fence every time. That's what the other team always expects you to do."

Everybody always played him at the base of the fence, 300 feet away. We had built the fence that far away mostly to keep line drives from getting lost in the weeds or the trees. Only four guys on our team had ever hit one over the fence at our own field.

I hit one on a windy day, a fly ball that seemed to go straight up and drop just a foot behind the fence. If the left fielder could have got there in time, he could have easily snagged it before it dropped over, but no one plays me that deep. I'm a singles and doubles hitter. It was a fluke.

Jimmy hit two, both boomers that surprised everyone, himself included. He's a big kid who hits a lot of long fly balls, but no one expected him to hit one that far, let alone two. Our guys still argue over whether the second one was fair or not. I don't argue because I know. I had been pitching, leading by 1 just before dark, a man on first. Jimmy's fly ball leaped off the bat and went skying down the left field line.

I knew it was gone when it left the bat. The only question would be whether it was fair or foul.

Ryan, who plays center field for us during the season, was in left because Andy was up after Jimmy for the other team. Ryan can fly. I mean, that kid can outrun any of us, and we have a few guys who have won track blue ribbons. Ryan dashed into the left field corner, his back to the infield.

I hurried to the third base line to watch the flight of the ball. I could see Toby digging around second, and even though he was the tying run for the "other" team, I was proud of him. I mean, we're all really on the same team, so in practice you want everyone to do the right thing. It was clear Ryan wasn't going to get to the ball, so it would be either a long foul ball, a home run, or an extra base hit that rolled to the fence.

If by some miracle Ryan caught up to it and hauled it in, Toby could have hustled back to first base without getting doubled up. Ryan may have been fast and had a fair arm, but he wasn't Superman. "Good hustle, Tob'!" I hollered as he rounded second. "Keep the play in front of you, and be ready to burn either way!"

The ball was still fair when it dropped over the fence. I had the best view of it of anybody on the field except Bugsy, who had been playing third base and was straddling the bag, hoping for a throw that never came.

Toby, steaming into third and watching the ball, began signaling fair ball, home run. But of course, he had a bad view. He was running full speed and was well to the right of the flight of the ball. Ryan flew into foul territory, wildly signaling foul ball. But of course, he had a bad view, too. When the ball went over the fence, he was running toward it from the right.

Bugsy immediately agreed with Ryan, but that was only because a home run would put him on the losing side. He knew as well as I did that the ball was fair. As usual, everybody looked to me to make the call. It wasn't that I was some kind of a know-it-all. They just trusted that I would be fair, no matter which team I was on. I was still standing on the third base line, staring into the corner where the ball had gone.

I jabbed my right arm toward the playing field, signaling a fair ball, but before I could even hear the cheering from the winners or the arguing and griping from my teammates, I was blind-sided by my first baseman, none other than big Jack. He ran into me so hard he knocked me ten feet off the baseline and into a heap.

At first I didn't know what had hit me. I might have been unconscious for a few seconds. I had a bruise on my arm and my ribs, and the wind was knocked out of me. I think Jack's head might have hit mine too, because I had a headache all night.

Well, I knew right off the bat that Jack had not run over me because he disagreed with the call. He just wasn't that type. He looked more scared than anybody else and kept apologizing. I wanted to tell him that it was all right and find out why he had done it, but I couldn't get enough air to say anything.

Finally, he explained. "You've been trying to teach me all this time and finally I got it and you were in the way!"

"In the way of what?" I managed.

"In the way of *me*," he said, pointing to himself. "Jack! Jack Bastable, the first baseman."

"He's right," Jimmy said. "Pitcher's supposed to be backin' up the catcher on that play with Toby more'n halfway to third. You've been drillin' it into Jack for weeks that he's supposed to line himself between the outfielder and the plate at about the distance of the pitcher's mound. He did, and there you were."

"I didn't mean to hurt you," Jack insisted. "I didn't hurt you, did I?"

"Well, yeah, you did. But I know you didn't mean to. It's all right. And you were right. You did the right thing. I was wrong."

Jack went from almost crying to smiling so widely he couldn't seem to quit.

Jimmy spoke up. "So what was the call again, Dal?"

I shook my head to clear it. "Fair ball. Home run." That time I heard the cheering and the griping. Ryan insisted that he had been the closest and had the best view. Toby insisted that I had been right, even though he had one of the worst views of the play. We still debate it. That was one of Jimmy's two homers.

It's hard to believe who the fourth guy is who has hit a ball over the fence at our park. Jimmy had two, I had one, Jack had four, and the other slugger had five. Ryan. Really. The smallest guy on our team and the fastest runner. He probably has the highest batting average too, just ahead of Bugsy and me.

There's just something about the bat speed little Ryan can generate. He's pale-skinned with whitish blond hair that somehow makes him look even smaller and younger than he is. He is only a year younger than most of us and a grade behind. But he was the first of us to hit a homer at our field. What a shock it was!

Bugsy was pitching that day, and he and Ryan had been arguing about who was the best. Bugsy claimed he was a better pitcher than Ryan was a hitter.

"This is the best way to find out," Ryan said, stepping in.

I could see that Bugsy was scared, because as good a pitcher as he is, I'd have to say that Ryan is better as a hitter. He's more consistent, better in the clutch.

The pressure was on. Bugsy would have to put up or shut up. I was playing short on Bugsy's team, so I jogged to the mound. "He looks pretty confident," I said.

"I know," Bugsy muttered. "Me and my big mouth."

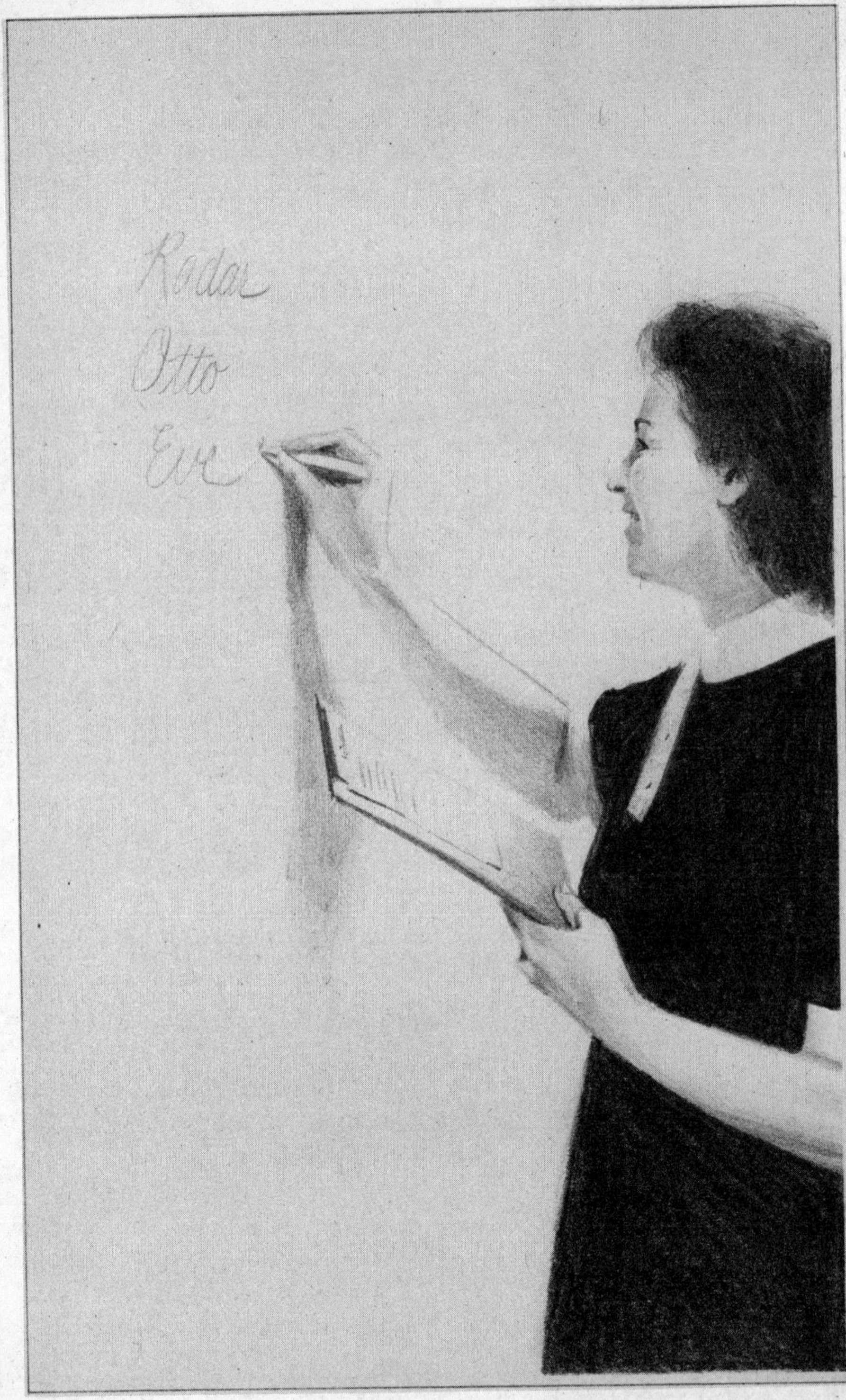
Radar
Otto
Eve

3

Back to School

"You really don't want him to show you up?" I asked Bugsy.

"Course I don't! What do you *think*?"

"Walk him," I said.

"Walk him? Are you kidding? That would be the worst."

"Worse than him driving one off you, maybe out of here?"

"No one has hit one out of *here*, Dal," Bugsy said. "I just want to get him out."

"I'm tellin' you, Bugs, I pitched to him in my yard yesterday, and he was hittin' my best stuff on the nose. I'd at least try to pitch around him."

Bugsy shook his head. "Dallas, there's nobody on and nobody out. I'm gonna look like a chicken."

The other guys yelled at us to get the game going.

"Just don't groove anything for him," I said, heading back to my position. "Pitch away from him a little."

Bugsy tried. His first pitch was a curve ball away, low and outside.

Ryan was motionless until he stepped directly toward the mound, bent his left knee, reached out, and snapped his wrists. I had never seen anything like it. That ball rocketed off and was a homer from the crack of the bat. Everyone on both teams just stood and watched it go, Ryan included.

He hit yet another homer in that game—off me this time—and for two weeks he was the only player in the club who had hit even one over our fence. He was still the leader, but now there were four of us. And I was facing Jack Bastable the day Mrs. Lucas had acted so strange in class.

Maybe that was on my mind and made me feel like a teacher. For whatever reason, I was coaching Jack. "First," I said, "a pitcher seeing you hitting in the cleanup spot and seeing your size will want to strike you out rather than risk trying to get you to hit into an out. Now, most will pitch you low and away first, probably showing you their fastball. Others will think you're expecting that and will pitch you up and in. That's what I'm going to do now, so be ready for it."

Jack smiled at me as if he thought I was kidding, that I wouldn't do exactly what I told him I would do. But that was a part of his lesson. I wanted him to see that sometimes a pitcher will do exactly what is expected in a given situation, and sometimes he won't.

When I threw a high hard one, in on Jack's chest just below his shoulder, he was stepping into the pitch as if he expected it to be outside. He ducked back and swung weakly at the same time.

I nearly fainted. If he hadn't reacted so quickly, he could have stepped right into the pitch and taken it in the head. "Jack!" I shouted. "I'm not trying to fool you! I'm trying to teach you! I wouldn't try to hurt you!" He stared at me, unsmiling but nodding. "Next I'm going to try to nip the outside corner, hoping you'll be a little shy about stepping into a fastball."

Even though he knew what was coming, it worked. He stood stock still as the pitch came in, and he flinched but didn't swing as it caught the outside corner.

"Strike two!" I hollered. "Now, if I was really facing a hitter like you in a game, I would waste a pitch. You know what that means?"

He nodded. "Yes, you'd throw a bad pitch, hoping I'd chase it and strike out."

"But I'm not going to do that now. I'm going to do what a smart pitcher should do. I've set you up for my curve by throwing two fast balls. I'm gonna throw either a pitch inside that curves over the plate, or a pitch down the middle that curves a little outside."

"Which one?"

"Well, I'm not going to tell you that much, Jack! Anyway, I don't know if I can be that accurate. I know what I'm going to *try* to do, but we'll see how successful I am. What are you supposed to do with a curve, Jack?"

"Move up in the box and hit it before it breaks."

"Right!"

He nodded, and I wound up and threw. My plan was to throw a strike that tailed off at the end. I snapped off the throw, and it headed straight at Jack. I was glad it was a curve and that I had given him fair warning. I was also glad he didn't panic and freeze, in case I hadn't put enough on the ball to make it curve across the plate.

Jack was ready. So ready that he wasn't about to let the pitch break. He stepped up and swung with all his might, not having been thrown off by my setting him up with two fast balls, because I had told him exactly what I was doing and what I would do.

I don't know how he did it, hitting an inside curve ball before it broke and making it come right back through the box, but he did. I'm telling you, it was a screamer. If I had had to think about it, I never would have got a glove on it. By instinct I flashed my glove out. The ball slammed off the heel of the glove and onto my right wrist, caroming high over the shortstop's head and into left field.

The ball dropped in safely, but as I turned to watch the play, I saw Jack running straight for the mound. "Are you all right, Dallas? I didn't mean to hit you!"

I didn't know if I was all right. I knew I was lucky I'd stuck my glove out, or that liner might have broken a rib. I looked at my wrist. Already welling up was a red and blue imprint of the threads of the ball. My hand throbbed, but I knew nothing was broken. "What a hit, Jack! Next time a pitcher sets you up oh-and-two with two fast balls, blast that curve right back at him."

He laughed. I knew he was relieved that I was all right. Everyone wanted to get a look at my wound before leaving for home.

Jimmy cycled home with me, and we got permission for him to eat with us, study with me, and stay overnight. We raced to his house to get some clothes, and the topic of conversation—until we fell asleep long after we should have—was Jack, my wrist, and of course, Mrs. Lucas.

By the time we got to school the next day, exhausted, Jimmy and I had a list of clues we thought we had detected in Mrs. Lucas's "performance" of the day before. The baseball imprint on my wrist was the center of attention before class began, but as soon as the bell rang and we were all settled, I raised my hand.

Mrs. Lucas was her old self. "Yes, Dallas?" she said, as if she expected something special from me. She always called on us that way, as if the greatest thing she could have ever taught us was to ask good questions.

"I was wondering if you could give us any more clues about the end of class yesterday."

I sensed a lot of my classmates nodding, but Mrs. Lucas looked puzzled.

"Tell me more," she said.

I didn't know what to say. She either didn't know what I was talking about, or she was pretending not to. It was clear she didn't want to give any more clues or even tell us what she had been up to. All Jimmy and I had were some ideas, but we couldn't be sure what she was driving at. The first thing we needed to do was to find out what kind of a puzzle or game or riddle we had on our hands. Then we had to keep track of the clues and try to come up with an answer. We'd done this before.

One day Mrs. Lucas had simply written several words on the board. She didn't tell us they all had something in common. She simply told us that she wanted one more word from each of us by the end of the day, and she gave us an hour to study in the library or discuss the problem with each other.

The words seemed to have nothing in common at first, but then it became clear to most of us. The words were radar, Otto, Eve, Hannah, and madam. Three proper nouns and two nouns that seemed to have nothing to do with each other. Denise, one of the smartest kids in our class, was the first to come up with the solution.

"Those words are the same, spelled backward and forward," she said. So the next question was what word Mrs. Lucas wanted from each of us. That stumped even Denise. She figured it would be yet another word that was the same spelled both ways, and we thought of plenty.

But Jimmy was the only one who got it right. He went to the library and looked in dictionaries and encyclopedias, finding nothing, then turned to the librarian, who directed him to a games magazine. In it he found the word *palindrome*, which means a word spelled the same backward and forward. That was the word he turned in at the end of the day. Even though he was the only one right, we all learned.

But now what? Mrs. Lucas was pretending not to know what I was talking about. Was that part of this new game? "When you didn't go through your normal routine at the end of the day," I reminded her. "That was the start of some sort of puzzle, right?"

She thought for a moment. "You know," she said, "I guess one day is starting to blend right in with the next, now that we're into our last full month of school. I honestly don't remember the end of the school day yesterday."

She sounded serious, but when I smiled at her, she winked at me. Another clue? Was her new word *amnesia*? Or *deception*?

Or *opposite*? Maybe that was it. This was opposite week. She would do exactly the opposite of what we expected. I mentioned that to Jimmy at recess.

"Too easy," he said. "I doubt it."

"Amnesia then?"

"You mean forgetting things?"

I nodded.

"I don't think so."

"Why not?"

"Why not what, Dal?"

"Why not amnesia?"

"I'm sorry, I forgot what we were talking about."

I punched him on the arm. "What is it then, Jim? We're getting nowhere."

4

Stumped

After four days without another clue from Mrs. Lucas, I almost forgot about the game. Either she was being very sly about her clues, or I had missed them altogether. She was her normal self: funny, fast-talking, and interesting. She was still strict, too. That was one thing she never let up on, even when we were having fun.

We all knew she was the boss. She had a way of keeping us in line with a look or a quiet word. Jimmy and I were talking once when she had asked everyone to be quiet and listen. All of a sudden we were aware that it was silent in the room except for our whispering. We looked up, and she was just staring at us.

She didn't appear upset, and after a second she started in on her lesson again. That's when I leaned over to Jimmy to quickly finish our conversation. As soon as I turned, I knew it had been a mistake. The whole classroom was silent again. I turned slowly back around to face her.

"Mr. O'Neil," she said quietly. "Are you quite through?"

"Yes, ma'am," I said, and I sure was.

After class, she asked to see me. "Dallas, I have known you since you were born, and I know you're a good kid from a good family. But I am not above embarrassing you in front of your friends, if that's what it takes to keep you in line. Do you understand?"

"Yes, and I'm sorry."

"I'm glad I didn't have to tell you that you owed me an apology. That just confirms the fact that I know you're basically a good boy. You're one of the smartest kids in my class and clearly a leader. That gives you a big responsibility. Kids look up to you, they follow you, they do what you do. That's great, as long as what you do is what they should be doing. When it isn't, I'm going to call you on it."

"You won't have to call me on it again," I said. I meant it. I wasn't going to give her another reason to have to hassle me. She did anyway, but it wasn't my fault. It really wasn't.

We were doing a science project, and, of all people, Denise did something before she was allowed. We all had been given thin strips of magnesium, which we held in safety tongs. When instructed, one at a time we were to light these. But there were precautions that had to be followed. There were only so many sets of dark goggles to go around, and the person lighting his magnesium was to wear a set, and so were those closest to him. Others in the room were either not to look directly at the burning strip or were to squint and just peek at it from a distance. It was bright enough to damage your eyes.

Well, for some reason Denise got it in her head that we were eventually supposed to light the thing, so she just went ahead and did it. Everybody oohed and aahed and pointed and made a big deal out of it, when all of a sudden Mrs. Lucas came storming into the middle of the group, holding goggles over her eyes.

"Don't look at it," she screamed. "Turn your eyes away! Denise! Drop it!"

Denise dropped the intensely glowing strip, and Mrs. Lucas kicked it around and stepped on it to try to smother the tiny ball of flame, which was not really possible—she explained later—until it had burned itself out. All she succeeded in doing was to get it out of most everyone's line of sight.

She was mad, and I mean real mad. That was obvious by how she set her mouth and refused to say anything except for a few commands. She made everyone turn in his magnesium strip, we skipped recess, and she lectured us.

"I was told by the principal that I should not do that experiment with a class under eighth grade," she said. "But I assured him you were the most mature sixth grade I had ever had. I told him that if there was a group of children anywhere in this state who could handle the responsibility of a dangerous experiment in the classroom, it was you people.

"But, you have let me down. You didn't wait for instructions. I know it was just as much my fault for not being clear about the danger and the precautions before we started, but I didn't expect you to proceed without permission and instruction. I just hope none of you have injured your eyes and impaired your vision for the rest of your lives, but now we will have to get a physician in here to find out."

And then, without warning, she began to cry. We had seen her cry before, but usually it was because of something moving or touching that happened in class. She cried when Bill Barnes told of his grandmother's dying, and she cried when Toby told about our winning the state track meet. She was that happy for us.

Now I thought she was crying because we might have injured ourselves in her experiment. We knew it was our fault, but we also knew that she would probably want to take all the blame for it because she could have prevented it. But that was not why she was crying. She wasn't crying for us. She was crying for herself, and I had never seen that before.

"You know, I'm not that far from retirement," she said.

That surprised me. I thought of that one time she had told us all the interesting dates in her life, like when she started school (she said it was back before kindergarten was popular, so she started in first grade), when she graduated from high school (at age eighteen), when she was married and had her kids, and all that. Then, later that day, she had asked everyone to guess her age.

She had given us enough clues to make it obvious she was in her late forties, and most everyone got it right. And now she was saying that she was not that far from retirement? I couldn't make that make sense. I thought teachers retired at sixty-five or seventy, and that was still more than fifteen years away, longer than I had lived already.

I raised my hand to question her about it, but she kept talking. "Now I've done this, after all these years in the classroom. I've injured some students, maybe blinded them. If even one of you has had his vision impaired, I'll be sued, maybe even prosecuted." She was sobbing now, and we didn't know what to think of it. "I'll lose my job, my pension, my retirement, my reputation, everything!"

I still had my hand up, but Mrs. Lucas rose and burst from the room. I wanted to tell her that I was sure none of us would blame her. We wouldn't let her take all the blame. At the door she whirled around and yelled at me, something else she had never done before.

"Oh, Mr. O'Neil, would you put your hand down! You always think you have something to say! Why don't you just admit that this was your fault, and that's the end of it!"

It wasn't common for me to talk back to my elders, but I couldn't help it. "*My* fault?" I said, looking around the room for help. Surely, no one else believed *that*. But not even Jimmy would look back at me. I saw kids squinting, rubbing their eyes, worried. She had scared them. Even if no one's vision had been affected, she had convinced most everyone that it could have been.

I wasn't going to get any help in my innocence when everyone was afraid of going blind. "*My* fault!" I repeated. "I didn't even light mine! I was one who turned my strip back in!"

36

"Don't lie to me, Dallas O'Neil! I know you were first and that you tried to put everybody else up to it just to get at me!"

I was speechless. Something was wrong with her! How could she say that about me? I would never do anything like that! "Mrs. Lucas!" But she was off down the hall, blubbering loudly.

I shook my head. "I don't believe this," I said.

"My eyes hurt," someone else said.

"Mine too! Denise, why did you do that?"

"Shut up!" Denise said. That wasn't like *her* either, but obviously we were all upset.

There wasn't the typical uproar there usually was when Mrs. Lucas was gone for a minute. In fact, when the principal, Mr. Garrison, came in, we were quiet, still sitting at our desks.

"Mrs. Lucas is pretty distraught," he said. "Would someone like to tell me what happened?"

No one volunteered, but a lot of the kids looked at me. I didn't know if they were trying to blame me or get me to tell the story.

"What did Mrs. Lucas tell you?" Brent asked.

"She told me she had passed out magnesium strips for an experiment, but that someone lit one before she could warn you all of the dangers."

"Yeah! She should have! Why didn't she? Are we all going to go blind?"

"Well, she should have told you. She admits that. And no, I don't believe you're going to go blind or even suffer any problems. As some of you know, my background is in the sciences, and I had something like this happen in a high school class many years ago. The person who lit his magnesium strip too early saw spots and suffered some pain for a few days, but his vision was restored perfectly.

"Just to be sure, my secretary is trying to arrange for a local eye doctor to come in this afternoon and test everyone, prescribing whatever is necessary. There will, of course, be no charge to any of you or your families. We will inform all of your parents and legal guardians of what happened. Are any of you experiencing any problems now?"

A couple of kids raised their hands, both complaining of pain.

"I need to tell you that pain at this point, unless you were within inches of the burning magnesium, is psychological. It's in your mind. The pain associated with this type of eye injury will not typically be felt until at least eight hours from the time it happened. Is anyone seeing spots or experiencing a blind spot?"

Denise raised her hand. "I am," she said. "If I close my left eye, I see a yellow spot in my right eye. And if I close my right eye, I have a blind spot in my left."

"And you were how far from the burning magnesium strip?"

Denise hesitated and looked at me.

5

A New Twist

Icouldn't believe this was happening. What was Denise looking at me for? Wasn't *anyone* going to believe me? Wasn't anyone going to remember that I hadn't lit my magnesium strip, that I had not followed Denise's example, that I had turned mine back in?

"I was the closest one to the burning strip," Denise told Mr. Garrison. "I was the one who went ahead without Mrs. Lucas's permission or instructions. It was my fault."

"Why, thank you, Miss—uh—"

"White," she told him. "Denise White."

"Well, Denise," he said, "that helps clarify a few things for me. You see, Mrs. Lucas was so upset that she couldn't remember who had been the first to go ahead. How many of you were close to Denise when she did this?" Several raised their hands. "And how many of you saw it burning from somewhere in the room?" We all raised our hands.

He asked if anyone else was seeing spots or experiencing blind spots, but apparently everyone had squinted or looked away when the strip started glowing white. "You'll all be tested as soon as possible after lunch, and my hope is to do it right here in the classroom."

I was still reeling from Mr. Garrison's saying that Mrs. Lucas had been confused and didn't know who had started the trouble. We all knew it was Denise, and I thought sure Mrs. Lucas knew that too. She was the first person Mrs. Lucas spoke to when everything started, and she told Denise to drop her strip. If it had been any other teacher, I wouldn't have been surprised that she might have forgotten, in all the confusion, exactly what had happened.

But then for Mrs. Lucas to blame me and to be so sure of it! It just didn't sound like her. Then she runs down the hall crying—which also wasn't at all like her—and tells Mr. Garrison she doesn't know who did it. I couldn't make any sense of it. Had I convinced her with my pleading that she had been mistaken? And then was it simply that, knowing it wasn't me, she returned to her confusion of not remembering who it was?

As if that didn't confuse me enough, I talked to Brent during lunch, and he said he saw Mrs. Lucas talking to Denise privately before the experiment.

"You're kidding," I said.

Jimmy and Brent sat across the lunchroom table from me. "Why?" Jimmy said. "What about it?"

"The whole thing could have been a setup," I said. "She tells Denise what to do, what symptoms to complain of, and that she is going to blame me. Then Denise is supposed to tell the truth and see how many kids complain of vision problems."

"So we're not actually going to have eye tests this afternoon?"

"Oh, we probably are," I said. "But maybe that's all part of the education, whatever it is."

"Sounds pretty far-fetched," Brent said, "but then she's done some pretty strange things to teach us before."

I nodded. "That crying scene though—man, she really convinced me."

"Me too," Brent said.

"I'm still convinced," Jimmy said. "You can't tell me she was putting on an act when she was telling you off, Dallas."

"You thought that sounded like her?"

"No, not at all. But she wasn't acting. No way. In fact, if I were you, I'd worry about my parents finding out."

"Well, I *am*! But don't forget I'm innocent."

Jimmy didn't say anything.

"Jimmy! You *do* know I was innocent, don't you?"

He shrugged.

"How can you say that?" I demanded.

"How can I say *what*?" he said. "I don't remember what everybody was doing when all that was going on."

"Yeah, but you know me and that I don't lie. You trust me. I said I didn't light one, and I didn't. I turned mine back in."

"Well, you keep saying that—"

"I keep saying that because it's true. You believe me, don't you?"

"I guess, but—"

"You *guess*? I'd believe *you, friend!*"

"C'mon, Dallas! She was standing there accusing you of having started it all and then all but calling you a liar when you denied it."

"But Denise has confessed to it!"

"Mrs. Lucas even accused you of doing it on purpose to get her, whatever that means."

"I'd like to know what that means, too," I said. "Do you think that sounds like something I'd do?"

Jimmy shrugged.

"Boy," I added, "you're some friend."

"Don't start with me, O'Neil. I just don't want to be on board when your ship goes down."

"It's not going down! I told you—and you heard it—Denise took the blame."

My heart nearly stopped beating when Mr. Garrison entered the lunchroom and looked around. When he spotted me, he headed straight for our table. Brent and Jimmy decided their lunch was over and slipped away.

"Better not go outside," Mr. Garrison called after them. "Let's be sure about those eyes first, OK?" They nodded and headed for the gym.

"Dallas, I need to talk to you," he said. "We have a local eye doctor and his assistant coming in at one to test everyone. Frankly, I don't think there will be any problems. I'm worried most about Denise, but those strips Mrs. Lucas used are so short and burn so quickly that I don't think permanent damage could have been done unless someone stared right at it from close range."

He hesitated, and I felt I should say something, but he hadn't asked me a question, and I didn't know what to say. He continued. "I need to tell you that you have a good reputation around this school. You know that, don't you?"

"I guess."

"Well, you do. Being a good student, active in sports, a church-going kid, and you've served—what—two years on the student council?"

"Three."

"Ah, well, there you go. Three. Good. Great. And that's why I need you to tell me exactly what happened in the classroom today."

I told him. And then I asked him why he needed to ask that after Denise had already told him.

"Well, son, Mrs. Lucas feels you were the cause of it."

"I know she *thinks* that, but it's like I told you. I mean, if Denise hadn't admitted it, I probably wouldn't have told on her. But it's the truth."

"Well, I need to talk to Denise, but—"

"She already admitted it, Mr. Garrison. In class. To you when you asked."

"I know that, but you see, when I told Mrs. Lucas that I had got to the bottom of it, she didn't agree. Telling her that Denise had admitted it only reminded her that yes, it was one of her brighter students, but she came back to you. She says you did it, and that you did it on purpose just to make her mad."

"I'd never do such a thing."

"But if you did, why would you? Do you have any reason to have it in for Mrs. Lucas?"

"No! She's my favorite teacher! Just the other day I was talking with a friend about how we have to organize something with the class to give her a special farewell present when we finish this year."

"That's nice. Many of the classes write notes all over the board for the teacher on the last day. Then one of them takes a picture of it and sends it to him later."

"I know. I—"

"In fact, last year, Mr. Knuth's class hid all the messages by pulling the maps down and—"

"I know, sir. I was in that class."

"Oh, well, then you know all that. Was that your idea?"

"Yeah."

"Fine. Why don't you do something like that for her this year?"

"We might do that, but we wanted to do something more, too. She's really something special. The best teacher most of us have ever had."

Mr. Garrison leaned back and took his glasses off, rubbing his eyes, then looking deep into mine. "I think we need to talk to Denise," he said.

"There's something I should tell you," I said. "About Denise."

I don't know what he thought I was going to say. Maybe he thought I was going to tell him something bad about her so I would have an excuse if she tried to put the blame on me. Regardless, he didn't want to hear it. "Let's just save it until we're talking with her directly, shall we?"

That was OK with me. I just wanted to know what Mrs. Lucas was talking to her about before the experiment. I certainly wasn't going to say anything bad about her. "Mr. Garrison, there is something important I need to ask you, and I'll understand if you can't tell me."

"What's that?"

"Is it possible that this is all part of something Mrs. Lucas is trying to teach us?"

"What do you mean?"

"I mean it's so out of character for her to get as mad as she did, to forget to give us an instruction, and then to actually forget who was responsible for the trouble."

"Well, what do you mean about her trying to teach you something?"

"That's her style. She uses all kinds of creative ideas and clues sometimes, making games and puzzles and riddles out of learning. Could this be one of those?"

"I can't imagine," he said. "It's possible, I suppose, but if she was faking being that upset, she convinced me. And we *are* going to the expense of having a professional come in here to test everybody. I think she could have gone about getting a guest speaker from the medical community in a little more conventional manner. No, I think this is a real crisis."

"The only reason I ask is that a few days ago, she acted strange in class, and then today before the experiment, someone saw Denise and Mrs.—"

"I'd really rather you not discuss another student with me without her being present," he said.

6

The Confrontation

We found Denise, and Mr. Garrison asked if she and I would join him in his office. That was the worst, because when you're seen going in or coming out of the principal's office, it can become the talk of the school..

My biggest fear was that Denise would go back on her story. Maybe she thought she was *really* going to get into trouble now, and she would agree with Mrs. Lucas that I was to blame. I didn't need this hassle just now. Of course, I never need to be accused of something I didn't do, but if this got to be a long, drawn-out affair, I was going to be late getting home. We had our first big practice game of the season this afternoon, against a group of all-stars from a nearby Little League.

Both teams were going to wear uniforms, and the game was going to be at their field, which was a first for us. It had taken the local Little League a long time to even get permission to play us, and they finally were allowed to only if they played at our field. But by now I guess our reputation had been built enough for people to know that we were for real, even though we didn't have a coach. We did have to sign a thing that said we were on our own as far as insurance and injuries and all that, but that was OK with us.

Well, Mr. Garrison set Denise and me down and began with her, for which I was glad.

"Denise, in class, when I asked who had been responsible for the problem, you said you had."

I held my breath.

"Yes," she said. "That's right."

"Why does Mrs. Lucas say it was Dallas?"

"I have no idea. He didn't light his. I saw him turn it in. And when I lit mine, Mrs. Lucas came running straight for me, telling me not to look at it, to drop it, to squint, and everything."

I let out a big sigh.

Mr. Garrison turned to me. "Is there any reason Denise would lie for you?"

"No! We're not best friends or anything, if that's what you mean. And we don't really know each other enough for me to have anything on her, like if she tells on me I tell on her or something like that. I think she's just telling the truth because it's the truth and because she's like that."

"Thank you, Dallas," she said, smiling at me.

Oh, no, I thought. *That's all I need. Now she thinks I'm sweet.*

"Kids," Mr. Garrison said, "there's something I need to ask you, and it needs to be totally confidential. You know what that means?"

I nodded.

"You mean we can't tell anyone," Denise said.

"Exactly right. And this is a big responsibility, because this is very important. Do you understand?"

We both nodded, and I wondered if Denise was thinking what I was thinking: that too many adults talk to sixth graders as if they're second graders.

Mr. Garrison continued. "If you were younger, I wouldn't be able to talk to you about this. I need to know—"

I raised my hand.

Mr. Garrison sighed, and I could tell he was irritated. "Yes, Dallas, what is it?"

"I don't mean to interrupt," I said, "but before you ask us whatever it is you have to ask us, I'm wondering if we could clear up that other thing I was talking to you about—you know, about Denise talking to Mrs. Lucas before the experiment. See, some of my friends noticed that, and we thought maybe it was Mrs. Lucas planning some sort of a trick, which she does sometimes to teach us, like I told you."

Mr. Garrison looked at Denise. "Did you talk to Mrs. Lucas before the experiment?"

"Yes, or rather she talked to me. She asked me how my father and my brother were doing."

"She knows them?"

"She *taught* them. She taught my dad in first grade more than twenty-five years ago, and she taught my brother in sixth grade three years ago."

"So there was nothing about that conversation that had anything to do with the experiment or some special learning technique of hers?"

"No, but there was something a little different about it. She asked me if it was my father or my brother who always forgot his boots and couldn't button his own coat. I told her I had no idea, but I guessed she was talking about my dad."

Mr. Garrison studied her. "Why did you assume that?"

"Well, I can't imagine my brother not being able to button his own coat in the sixth grade. I mean, I can't imagine my father having that problem, either, but I suppose when he was in first grade it was a different story."

Mr. Garrison just sat looking at her. "Anything else?" he said finally.

She shook her head.

"Well," he said, "that leads back to what I wanted to talk to you about in confidence. Frankly, I'm a little worried about Mrs. Lucas just now. She seems to be going through some personal trauma or problem. While the ordeal today was serious, and I would say that her reaction to it would have been normal had she been any other teacher on my staff, for *her* it was an over-reaction. Did either of you feel that way?"

"She scared me—that's all I know," I said. "I mean, she convinced me that what had happened was really serious and that some of us could lose our vision. I had never seen her that upset, and she seemed scared. That rubbed off on us, I think."

Denise nodded. "I was a little surprised when she started raving about losing her job and all that. Normally, she would have been more worried about us than herself. She said something about retiring, too, which surprised me. I thought only old people retired."

"What did she say about retiring?" Mr. Garrison asked.

"Something about not being far from retirement. How old *is* she, anyway?"

"Well, I don't know right off, but I don't think she's fifty yet. That *is* a problem. Has there been anything else like that recently that has made you wonder about her?"

I told him about our usual procedure at the end of the day, and what she had done four days before about not letting us go and then reminding us about our wraps.

He nodded slowly. "You know, kids, there are a lot of things happening to a woman at Mrs. Lucas's age, and sometimes that results in strange comments or puzzling behavior.

"She seems very emotional and maybe nostalgic, so I'm going to ask you two—as leaders in your class—to help support her. Not by talking about this to anyone, because that would be unfair to her. But if and when she does something else that may appear funny or strange to your classmates, just support her, say good things about her, remind your classmates what a good teacher she has been, and see if you can't influence them to give her a break. One thing she doesn't need right now, if I'm right, is to be made fun of."

"What about the fact that she still thinks I'm responsible for what happened?" I asked.

"That *is* a problem, because she is convinced of it. I think I'd like to have Denise go to her—if you're willing, Denise—and apologize for your part in the incident. If that doesn't satisfy her, Dallas, I'd like you to do the same."

"But I—"

"I know you had nothing to do with it."

"Then what do I say? I can't say I did something I didn't."

"But you can apologize for having upset her."

"But *I* didn't upset her!"

"No, but she *thinks* you did. So, without being specific, just apologize for your part in upsetting her and leave it at that. She is upset at you for some reason, or for no reason—I don't know. Regardless, for whatever reason, she is unhappy with you. It doesn't make sense, and it doesn't have to make sense. Just do it for the sake of peace and harmony and see what happens."

"Then should I come back later this afternoon and tell you what she says?"

"Only if necessary."

When we returned to class, the eye doctor and his assistant were there, and the kids were all lined up. They had set up portable walls so their lighting equipment would work better. We stood at the back of the line.

When Mrs. Lucas noticed us, she said, "Oh, Dallas and Denise, I'm glad you're back. You'll never believe what happened. We had an experiment go wrong, and it was all my fault. Now we have to have everyone's eyes tested. You weren't here, so you don't need the test, but you might as well have it, since it's free."

A chill ran through my body, and I could see that Denise was scared too. A few of the other kids heard what she had said, and one—a big dark-haired kid named Trevor—spoke to her as if she had lost her mind.

"What're you talkin' about, Miz Lucas? They was the ones who started all this! Denise lit off her magnesium thing before you said, and you said Dallas done the same thing!"

"Watch your grammar, Trevor!" Mrs. Lucas snapped. "And get back in line!"

Trevor shrugged and turned away.

"I do want to apologize for what I did, Mrs. Lucas," Denise said, her voice quavery. "I didn't wait for your instructions, and I'm sorry."

Mrs. Lucas stood smiling at her, but the look on her face made it appear that she didn't understand.

I should have waited before I said anything, but I was so shaken by what she had said when we came in that I just blurted, "I'm sorry, too, for whatever I did that upset you."

"Dallas," she said, "you don't ever have to apologize for anything. You have been a model student of mine all year."

I froze. At least, and I mean at the very least, Mrs. Lucas had lost her memory. I had a feeling I was going to be late getting home that afternoon.

7

Two Victories

I knew I had to stop in and see Mr. Garrison before I went home, and I only hoped that it wouldn't take long.

Denise and I were the last ones to get our eyes checked. The doctor and his assistant were doing it two people at a time, so I was checked by the assistant—who found no problem with me—and I could hear the doctor checking Denise.

"Now, you were closest to the magnesium flash, correct?" She nodded.

"And, let me guess, you were holding it in your left hand and lit it with your right. Am I correct?"

"Yes, how did you know?"

"I see more temporary trauma in your left eye, the one closest to the flash. You're seeing spots or experiencing blind spots?"

"Yes."

"Both?"

"Yes."

"Probably a blind spot in the left eye and a white or yellow one in the right?"

"Exactly. Yellow. It's like I can still see the strip burning."

"Did you squint?"

"Yes, I knew enough to do that. And then Mrs. Lucas came running so fast and telling me to drop it that I think I only saw about half of it burn."

"I brought a welder's mask," the doctor said, "and I watched one of those burn. It lasts a little over five seconds. If you squinted when you watched it, you shouldn't have any long-lasting trouble. Your eyes may burn or ache later, probably only the left one. I'm prescribing some drops. If you are still experiencing pain tomorrow at this time, be sure to give me a call."

"How about the others? Were anyone's eyes injured?"

"Not that I could tell. You were all very lucky."

"Yeah, I know. And it was my fault. I don't know why I did that."

"Oh, it wasn't your fault."

"Yes, it was."

"Your teacher told me that she had not given the proper instructions. She feels terrible."

"I know, but I should have waited."

"She told me you lit yours and that you were closest to it, but she didn't seem to blame you."

"Well, I'm to blame."

The rest of the afternoon was spent with Mrs. Lucas reading us a story. She shut the shades and allowed those who wanted to to close their eyes. So, there we sat in a dark room, Mrs. Lucas reading to us by a small lamp on her desk.

For some reason, whenever I have my eyes closed during the day, I feel like praying. I kept losing track of the story she was reading because I was praying for her. Something was happening to her, and I didn't know what it was. I supposed that it still could have been a trick she was playing on us, but that didn't seem likely anymore. Jimmy and I were going to list all the clues, but by now there were so many that I couldn't keep up. Anyway, I didn't think I'd forget anything that had happened today.

What was so strange was how calm Mrs. Lucas was now. It was as if she was so relieved to find out everyone was OK that she relaxed and was her old self again. She told jokes as she read, made comments that made us laugh, even changed the story enough to find out if we were really listening.

When she was finished reading, she turned half the lights back on, asked how everyone felt, then told us what a great class we were. She singled our several students who had been doing well lately, including Denise and Jimmy and Brent and even Trevor. (She could always think of *something* positive Trevor had done, even though he would have had to be considered the bottom student in our class.)

But that was like Mrs. Lucas. She was always encouraging everybody. She was quick and witty and nice. With about ten minutes to go till the end of the day, she gave us some advice about not reading in low light, not looking directly into the sun, and how to tell our parents what had happened. "They've already gotten a call from the office, but you'll want to fill them in completely. Do tell them to call me directly if they have any problems.

"I'm terribly sorry I did not give full instructions, and I'm not holding this against anybody. Now, for some good news: I want you to postpone your homework from tonight to this weekend. Don't anyone take a book home tonight."

We all cheered, and she smiled. Then she quieted us with the smallest wave of her hand, like always. At three twenty-nine, she glanced at the clock and nodded to us. We put our books away and sat still until the bell rang. In the middle of the ring she nodded with a smile, and we were out the door.

She had been so normal, so like herself, that I almost wanted to forget about visiting Mr. Garrison again. But I couldn't. I wanted to tell him everything that had happened since I left him and let him make his own decision about what it all meant.

He was glad I had come to him. He looked troubled when I told him what she had said about my not having had anything to do with it and not needing to apologize. Then he seemed pleased with how the day had turned out. "Dallas, thank you for bringing me up to date. I think this is good news, very good news. I don't want to pretend that Mrs. Lucas hasn't been very puzzling for us today, but I'd like to give her the benefit of the doubt.

"You know, she has been teaching in this district since her senior year at teachers' college, and she has been a very loyal, trusted, and honored member of our staff. Let's chalk this off to a very tense, distressing situation and assume that she's back to being herself. What do you say?"

I shrugged. "It's OK with me. I still wonder what happened the other day at the end of the day, though."

"I think she was probably simply daydreaming and lost track of the time."

"Maybe, but that's sure not like her. Today she thought she had cost herself her job, and by the end of the day she was back on schedule with her signals and everything. And that line about our wraps—"

"You're sure you didn't misunderstand that?"

"I'm sure. Denise and Jimmy heard it too."

"That only convinces me she was thinking about something else, was remembering something from a previous school year, maybe had wintertime on her mind. All right?"

"Sure."

"She used to teach the younger grades, you know. For more than ten years she taught kindergarten and first grade."

"Did she?"

He nodded. "That's where you have to help all the kids with their coats and boots and things."

"Yeah, and where winter clothes are called wraps."

He laughed and clapped me on the knee. "Exactly! Now, if you'll excuse me, we'll see if we can get this building emptied in time for the staff to go home."

That was good news for me. I could still make it home in time for the game. I'd probably be the last to show up, which would be strange. Usually I was first, because I brought all the equipment. And tonight I was pitching. I pedaled home as fast as I could.

When I passed Jimmy's house, he was already coming out with his uniform on. "Dallas! Where you been?"

I knew I couldn't tell him I had been talking with Mr. Garrison about Mrs. Lucas, so I just said I had something to do after school.

"You'd better get going to the game," he added.

"I know," I hollered. "How about takin' the equipment for me?"

"Sure!"

He followed me home, and we slid into my driveway in a cloud of gravel and dust. He slung the canvas bag of bats and catcher's equipment over his handlebars and rode off toward the highway, and I got out of my school clothes and into my uniform in record time. For the first time in months, I let the screen door slam. I knew I would hear about that later.

The way we played that afternoon, and the fact that a lot of families from both teams showed up to watch, made me feel great. The Little Leaguers put a lot of emphasis on pitching and defense, and we always had trouble scoring against them. But the deepest part of their fence was only 210 feet to center field, so a couple of fly balls that would have been easy outs on our field carried for homers against them.

I felt so good about the change in Mrs. Lucas and had been so fired up by hurrying home that I was ready to pitch. We batted first, and, after Ryan led off with a bunt single and advanced to third on Brent's ground out, I bounced the first pitch off the right center field fence for a sliding double.

The pitch had been high and outside and would probably have been a ball, but I had such a good look at it that I couldn't resist. The pitcher was fast and usually accurate, so I had decided that if I got anything close that was good to hit, I'd pull the trigger.

I was surprised that I had to slide, but I had taken my eye off the play as I rounded first. In fact, in turning to make sure that Ryan scored—he'd waited because there was a chance one of the fielders might have caught up with my fly ball—I nearly overran first base, catching the edge of it with my heel. When I looked back up, the center fielder was wheeling around with the throw. A good peg would have nailed me, but it came in about shoulder high on the shortstop, and I slid in under the tag.

Later in the game, with the outfield pulled in on our tiny lead off man and the infield remembering his bunt single from the first inning, their pitcher grooved one that Brent hit almost in the same spot as my double. The only difference was that his had a little more on it and cleared the fence.

Later yet, Jack hit what appeared to be a high foul ball down the first base line, but it cleared the 175-foot marker in right, and when we could convince Jack it had been fair, he trotted around for our second homer.

We won 6-2, and I allowed just six hits, one home run. I felt great. The team was playing well. Mrs. Lucas was back to normal. Maybe my prayers had been answered the way I wanted.

At least I thought so until the following Monday.

8

Blue Monday

Some kids don't like Mondays because it means getting back to school and responsibilities. I sort of look forward to Mondays. I always spend the day before in church with my friends and some people I see only at church. I like Sunday school and even the morning service, most of the time.

That Sunday I did a lot of praying about Mrs. Lucas, mostly thanking God for the fact that she seemed all right again. I did have a strange thought at the back of my mind that I was really only hoping she was OK. Just because she was back to normal for a while didn't mean she would never act odd again.

When she went four days without doing anything out of the ordinary, I tried to forget what had happened at the end of that school day, the first time she acted strange. Just when I had decided that it had either been my imagination or it was simply an old woman thinking about something else and losing track of the time, she was worse than ever.

I know it was set off by that science experiment, but still, she was so unlike herself. I tried to imagine how she would have handled it earlier in the year. First of all, she would never have passed out magnesium strips and matches to everyone at once. She probably would have done the experiment herself first, telling us to wear protective goggles or to squint or look away, and showing us how to do it.

Then we probably would have done the lighting one or two at a time, with her continually reminding us how to do it safely. Then, if something had gone wrong, she would have taken the guilty person out in the hall and given him or her a lecture that wouldn't quit. And that would have been the end of it.

The way it happened, she upset everyone, herself included. She was like a mad woman, ranting and raving, saying things that didn't make sense, accusing innocent people, forgetting who did what and even who she *thought* was guilty. From one minute to the next, we had no idea what she might say or do. It felt so good by the end of the day to have her back to normal. I was praying she would stay that way.

I had learned a long time ago not to think that God has to answer my prayers the way I want Him to. I prayed that my grandmother would not die, but she died anyway. It took me a long time to figure that one out, and for a while I didn't understand God too well. I didn't think I liked Him, either. I was six when we found out Grandma had cancer, and she was terribly sick for almost a year before she died.

My parents took me to see her a few times, but I could hardly stand it. She slept most of the time, and there were awful medicine smells and tubes running everywhere. Finally it got to the point where she had one machine that breathed for her and another that fed her. She was in constant pain, so they had to keep giving her shots so she wouldn't be so miserable.

I prayed and prayed and prayed that God would make her better, and when she died I thought He hadn't answered my prayers. My mother said she didn't want her mother to suffer any longer. I said I didn't either and that's why I prayed she would get better.

"She got better," Mom said.

"Why did she have to die?" I asked.

"We all have to die, Dallas. She was ready. She believed Jesus had died for her sins, and she had received Him by faith. I know she wanted to watch you and your sisters grow up, but even more, she wanted to be with Jesus. She's healthier now than she's ever been. God did answer your prayers. You thought you were praying that she wouldn't die, but you were really praying that she would get better. She's not suffering now."

"But I miss her, and I want her back."

"So do I, honey, but that wouldn't be what's best for Grandma, would it? That would be what is best for us. It would be selfish of us to make her come back from heaven now."

"I still feel like crying."

"So do I. And I will. I'll miss her terribly, and I'll remember all that she taught me and all the wonderful things she did for me all these years. Every time I feel like crying because I miss her, I'm going to do just that. And I'm going to be reminded to thank God that He took her before she had to suffer more. I'm going to thank Him for all she meant to us. And you know what else I'm going to thank Him for?"

"What?"

"That He died for her sins so she wouldn't have to be punished. And that He died for my sins and yours, which means that someday we will get to see Him and who else?"

"Grandma."

So now how was I supposed to pray for Mrs. Lucas? I wanted her to get better. I didn't want her to embarrass herself or suffer, but what if God wanted *her* to come to heaven too? This certainly didn't seem like anything that would kill a person, but who knew how crazy she might get? There, I said it. I worried that she might be going crazy. She was sure doing strange things.

I got to school that Monday morning in a pretty good mood. The homework she had told us to put off from Thursday night to the weekend was done. The Baker Street Sports Club was excited about having beaten the Little League all-stars. Church had been fun. And—I hoped—Mrs. Lucas would be her old self.

Everything was going fine in the morning until it was time for recess. We were five minutes past the time when we were supposed to go outside. That may not sound like much, but we were eager to get going. It was a nice, sunny day, and we had two innings of a softball game to play against the other sixth grade team. We could see them out on the diamond warming up.

Every time Mrs. Lucas turned her back to write on the board or point to a map or chart, kids started whispering, trying to get my attention. They wanted me to raise my hand and remind her that it was time to go outside. I ignored them. I didn't want to do it. And I was dying inside.

A five-minute mistake by Mrs. Lucas was unusual. She had always been right on time, exactly to the minute. It didn't make sense. When she strolled over to the window, still talking, she noticed the playground full of kids. The upper grades—fourth, fifth, and sixth—all had recess together.

Suddenly she stopped in the middle of a sentence and whirled around. "Why, what time is it?" she asked.

No one answered because the clock was in the center of the wall above the board, and she was closer to it than anyone else. And when we were late for recess or lunch or going home, that clock seemed to grow and cover the whole front of the room. Besides, Mrs. Lucas wore a watch. She knew well enough what time it was. We all just sat and stared at her.

She looked at the clock, then at her watch, then at us. Maybe because none of us were saying anything or complaining, she was confused. "Have you already been outside?" she asked.

I was stunned, but few others seemed to be. Such a question made it impossible for me to speak, I was so scared. How could she ask such a thing? How could she really not know that we had been sitting there in her class for two hours already? What did she mean, have we been outside yet?

I could have lived with that little lapse—it was nothing really, except that it was Mrs. Lucas, who never made such mistakes. She should have said, "Oh, I'm sorry I went overtime. Hurry outside, and I'll call you in a few minutes later." But she didn't. She turned on us. Fortunately for me, she didn't blame me. But I always take the scolding personally, since she had told me what a leader I was and how much responsibility I had.

"Why didn't anyone tell me it was time for recess?" she demanded. She didn't look at me, but still her question burned through me. Had it come to this? Would one of us be required to remind her every time the clock said we should be doing something different?

"Huh?" she repeated. "Am I supposed to keep track of our entire schedule all by myself? Will no one else in this class take any responsibility? Do I have to be your baby-sitter? You're going to regret this, because I'm going to have to punish you. You'll just skip recess this morning and see how you like that. Maybe next time someone else will take some responsibility for the class here. Let's just continue then."

But in continuing, she was still not herself. She had been rattled, as we had, and she kept interrupting herself to scold us. I knew she was embarrassed that she had forgotten, and she was trying to put the blame on someone else. But that was the type of thing a kid would do, not a teacher.

"Someday," she said, "and it's not too many years from now, you'll be in junior high school, and then you won't have a teacher who has to act like your mommy too."

What was she saying? We would be junior highers in just four months! She was treating us like little kids again, like she thought we were first graders. But would she really expect first graders to tell her what time it was and that it was time to go outside?

69

I decided to try something. I knew it didn't make a lot of sense, but then neither did she, so it was worth a try. I raised my hand.

"Yes," she said. "What is it?"

"Mrs. Lucas, I'm sorry I didn't tell you when it came time for recess, but I didn't think anyone would mind if we were a little late getting outside."

I expected one of two reactions. Either I would convince her and she would be flattered and forgiving, or I would irritate her and she would be madder than ever. I was wrong. She didn't react either way. She just stared at me and then at everyone else in the class, one by one.

I heard Trevor mutter, "O'Neil, you're nuts," and Mrs. Lucas glared at him as if he had said it about her. Then she continued searching the eyes of everyone in the room. Most of the kids glanced away when she looked at them, then looked back when she was looking elsewhere.

Denise, however, stared right back into her eyes. At first I thought she was being defiant, but the more I looked at Denise, the more fear I saw on her face. Like me, she had no idea what to do or say.

When Mrs. Lucas quit staring at us, she went and sat at her desk. She rested her chin in her hands and stared blankly into space for a while, then she sat up straight and folded her hands in her lap, as if she were listening to a concert recital or something. She just stared ahead.

Kids were looking to me to do something. I raised my hand. She didn't look at me, though I know she could see my hand. I left it up. Then Denise raised hers. Then Jimmy. Then two others. And there we sat, with an hour and a half to go until lunch time, the sixth grade class of Mrs. Lucas, sitting there with our hands raised while she sat motionless at her desk.

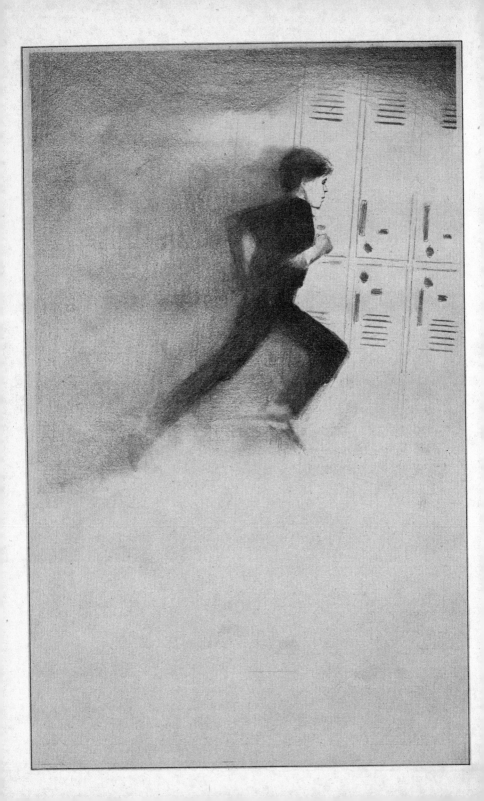

9

The Deadlock

I felt almost as if I was defying Mrs. Lucas by sitting there with my hand up for so long. She continued to ignore me and everyone else, and I had to prop up my arm with my other hand. Some of the others started waving, but I would not do that. I knew she saw us. After four or five minutes, one by one we lowered our hands.

"Mrs. Lucas," one of the girls said quietly, fear in her voice. There was no response.

"What're we s'pose to do now, O'Neil?" Trevor asked.

I shrugged. "Whatever we want, I guess." I said it loud enough that Mrs. Lucas could hear it and she could scold me for it if she wanted. At that point I would have done anything to get a response from her. She said nothing. She didn't even move. I pulled out a book and began reading. Several others did the same.

Some talked quietly with each other, and the longer Mrs. Lucas let that go on, the more they did it. An hour passed. A girl next to Denise whimpered, "Is Mrs. Lucas sick?"

"How should we know?" Trevor asked. "If she ain't movin' by lunch time, I'm outta here. We got our rights, ya know, and one of 'em is to eat lunch. Come lunch time, state law says we get to go eat."

"What do you know about state law?" I asked.

"It's a fact, O'Neil," he said. "I don't know if it's state law or what, but I know she can't keep us in here through lunch time."

By now several kids were discussing the problem aloud, and Mrs. Lucas could easily hear us. Since she hadn't hassled anyone, it was as if she wasn't there, and everyone got confident that she wasn't going to discipline them. A few kids even got up and walked around the room. Others started telling jokes and laughing.

Finally I stood and asked everyone to return to their desks. "I think we need to talk about this," I said.

"Forget talking," Trevor said. "Let's beat it."

"No, we can't beat it," I said. "Mrs. Lucas is not herself. Clearly she's not herself. If she was just trying to discipline us, she would have told us exactly what we had done wrong, what the punishment would be, and then she would have made us sit still and be quiet or read or something."

"Shouldn't you try to talk to her?" Denise suggested.

"I've tried." I faced the front of the room again and called out, "Mrs. Lucas, ma'am, may I ask you something?" There wasn't even the flicker of a response. "OK," I said, turning back to the class. "If she's still like this at lunch time, I think we should all leave quietly. I'll go get Mr. Garrison and tell him what's going on. I don't think we should tell anyone else what's gone on here."

"Are you kiddin'?" Trevor said. "This is the best thing that's happened to me this year! I'm gonna tell all my friends!"

"That won't take long," Denise said. "You're down to two now, aren't you?"

"Real funny, Denise."

"Well, quit being such a jerk, Trevor," Denise said. "Dallas is right. This will get around soon enough. We have to be loyal to our own teacher, don't we? She's been good and loyal to us, especially to you, Trevor. You have to admit she's treated you better than any other teacher we've ever had."

Trevor shrugged and didn't say anything, which was his way of reluctantly agreeing.

Peggy, a tiny girl in the back row, raised her hand. "Is Mrs. Lucas going to die?"

Trevor shook his head and sighed.

"I don't know," I said. "I don't know what's wrong with her."

"Well, I don't think we should wait any longer," Peggy pleaded. "I think you should go get Mr. Garrison now."

I looked at Mrs. Lucas. She just sat there. "Maybe you're right," I said. "It's as if she can't see or hear us." I was scared. I walked right up to her and leaned toward her, my hands at the edge of her desk. "Mrs. Lucas," I said. No response. "I'm going to go to the office and get Mr. Garrison to come and help you. OK?" Still nothing.

I turned back to the class. "Please just stay in your seats and don't make any loud noise or anything. I'll be right back." A chill ran through me as I left, shutting the door quietly and noticing that she still sat there as she had for more than an hour. As soon as I was out of sight of the door, I ran.

There's a rule in our school: no running indoors. I didn't care. This was an emergency. I raced down the hall, slid around the corner, bounded down a short flight of stairs, turned right and ran the length of the corridor to the school office. As I neared the door, a teacher was coming out.

"Stop running, young man!" she said.

I ignored her and ran into the office, only to find it full of people on various errands. There were a few men in business suits, two couples, and three or four students waiting in line to talk to the woman at the counter. Beyond her I could see the principal's secretary and the door leading to his office.

"Excuse me," I said from the back of the line. Several people turned and glared at me. I ignored them. "Ma'am, I need to see Mr. Garr—"

"I'm sorry, son," she said, "but there are several ahead of you here."

"To see Mr. Garrison?" I asked.

"Well, I don't know," she said sternly. "A few of them, I'm sure."

Two men and a couple turned and nodded to me. They wanted to see him too.

"Well, this is an emergency," I said.

"So is ours," the couple said. The wife added, "We had cleared an absence in advance, and now it's been marked against my daughter's record."

"I'm talking about a real emergency," I said, but I didn't want to tell anybody but Mr. Garrison.

"Has someone been injured?" the woman at the counter said. "Or are they sick?"

"Well, I don't know. Not exactly."

"Because if someone is sick or hurt, you know where the nurse's office is."

"No, I really need to see the principal."

"Then you'll just have to wait your turn," she said.

"Yeah," others in line chorused. "Wait your turn."

I waited another minute while the woman took care of yet another person's problem, a minor one compared to mine. Then I pushed past everyone and got to the counter, feeling very foolish and also very hated.

"Hey!" several said.

"Excuse me," I said. "I'm sorry."

"Did your teacher send you here?" the woman said.

"Well, no, not exactly."

"Does she know you're here?"

"Well, I told her, if that's what you mean."

"Of course that's what I mean. Did she send you here?"

"Hey, let the kid wait his turn. *Make* him wait."

"No, ma'am, I can't say that she sent me here, no."

"Please, I'm going to have to ask you to wait at the end of the line."

I looked past her to Mr. Garrison's secretary, who looked up at me and smiled. I looked at the end of the line. Three more people had come in. It would be longer than ever if I went to the end of the line again. Right in front of me was the section of counter that raised to allow people to walk through. I slipped under it.

"Hey!" the woman shouted. "Come back here!" She made a lunge for me and pulled my shirttail out, but I scooted away from her and tumbled into Mr. Garrison's secretary's office. The other woman gave up on me and turned back to the line at the counter.

I leaped to my feet and tucked my shirt in. "I'm sorry, Miss Lansing, but I need to see Mr. Garrison. It's sort of an emergency, but I really can't tell anyone but him."

"You spoke to him last week, didn't you?"

I nodded.

"He mentioned how much he enjoyed that and how impressed he was with you and, uh, the girl—"

"Denise."

"Right. Well, I know if you think it's important, he would see you right away."

I started to walk toward his door.

"However," she said, stopping me. "He's not in just now."

"Oh, no."

"Well, he's in the building, but not in his office. Can you give me an idea how important it is so I'll know whether or not to interrupt him?"

"I can't tell you. You'll just have to trust me."

"OK," she said. "I'll try. Have a seat."

I sat in a big chair next to her desk. She dialed and put her hand over the mouthpiece. "He's with Coach Schultz." She turned back to the phone. "Hi, Jenny. Is my boss in with yours? No? In the gym? OK, I'll just page him. Thanks." She hung up and started to dial again.

"Listen," I said, "don't page him. Just let me run down and find him. If you page him to come to the office, all those people will see him and know that I got to him before they did."

"Well, it's all right with me if you want to run down there. I don't know how long he's going to be. He could be on his way back by now."

"I'll check." I rose.

"You'll have to go back out the way you came, you know."

"I know," I said, sighing. "Maybe you could get me past the counter."

She smiled. "Sure."

Miss Lansing walked me back to the counter, and as people backed away, she lifted the movable section and let me through. She walked me all the way to the door and winked at me as I headed off down the hall. I broke into a run again as soon as I could. I knew that flying past open classroom doors would bring teachers out to see what was going on, but I was worried about Mrs. Lucas. I didn't know what was wrong with her or how important speed was.

I found Mr. Garrison huddled with Mr. Schultz on the first row of the bleachers. Neither man noticed me at first. When Mr. Garrison saw me, I went right up to him and spoke in his ear. "Sir, it's Mrs. Lucas. You need to come right now."

"Excuse me, Coach," Mr. Garrison said. "I'm sorry. I'll get back to you."

I filled him in on what was happening as we jogged through the school. When we got to the sixth grade classroom, the students were sitting there talking casually.

Mrs. Lucas was gone.

10

The Search

Mr. Garrison glanced at his watch. "Almost lunch time," he said. He strode into the classroom. "Students," he began, "where is your teacher?"

"She said she was going to lunch," Denise said. "She said she had punished us long enough for not reminding her it was time for recess, and now all we had to do was sit here until the lunch bell rings."

"How long ago was this?" As he spoke, the bell rang.

"Jes' after Dallas left," Trevor said.

"How long ago was that?" Mr. Garrison asked me.

"Less than ten minutes," I said.

"*Fewer* than ten minutes, you mean."

"Pardon me?"

"Nothing. I'm sorry. Once a grammarian always a grammarian. All right, students, you may go quietly to lunch."

The kids jumped from their seats.

"Quietly!"

Mr. Garrison didn't tell me I had to go to lunch, too, so I stayed with him. He didn't seem to mind, so I didn't ask if it was all right. "I have to page Mrs. Lucas," he said. He rang the intercom button at the front of our classroom.

"Office!" came the reply. It was the woman at the counter, and she sounded as busy as when I had been in there.

"This is Mr. Garrison. Would you please page Mrs. Lucas for me?"

"In her room?"

"No, I'm *in* her room. Page the whole building, and ask her to return to her room, please."

"Every room, all at once?"

"Yes!"

"Yes, sir."

In a second or two, when he hadn't heard the page, he buzzed her back. "Do it now, please!"

"Yes, sir."

"Mrs. Lucas. Paging Mrs. Lucas. Please report to your classroom immediately! Thank you!"

We waited about a minute, then Mr. Garrison buzzed the office again. "One more time, please."

When the second page brought no result, Mr. Garrison hurried back to his office with me close behind. In the outer office even more people stood in line, now including several students. Mr. Garrison breezed past everyone without a greeting, lifted the counter section for us both to walk through, and I followed him. As he passed his secretary he said, "Linda, please call Mrs. Lucas at her home. If you get no reply, get Mr. Lucas on the phone for me as soon as possible."

"Sir, there are two—"

"Right away please, Linda. We have a bit of a crisis here."

She turned to her phone and began dialing, but as we got into Mr. Garrison's office, it became obvious what she had been trying to tell him. Two men sat there with briefcases. They immediately rose and stuck out their hands. "Nice to meet you, Mr. Garrison. We're from Statewide School Supply, and we have several exciting propositions for you."

"Gentlemen," he said, shaking their hands briefly, "I'm afraid this is the worst possible time for us to talk. We—"

"Sir, Mr. Jennings and I will ask only a few moments of your time. Let me just show you—" He was trying to get his briefcase open, but Mr. Garrison had taken him by the arm and was guiding him toward the door.

"I know we had an appointment today, gentlemen, and I'm terribly sorry that an emergency has arisen that will make it impossible for me to talk to you just now. I would recommend that you make an appointment with my secretary first thing tomorrow morning. I'll appreciate your sensitivity."

"Mr. Garrison," Linda Lansing said over the office intercom, "I have Mr. Lucas on your line."

"Thank you. Excuse me, gentlemen." They didn't look too happy, but they left. Mr. Garrison signaled for me to shut the door, and as I did I heard them trying to arrange an appointment for the next morning.

Mr. Garrison stood with the receiver to his ear and parted the blinds in his office. "Mr. Lucas, your wife's car is gone from the parking lot. She told her students she was leaving for lunch about ten minutes ago, and frankly I'm worried about her. She has not been acting herself lately, and it's very much unlike her to leave her students unattended in the classroom. . . . Oh, you have? I wasn't aware of that, no. . . . Well, yes, maybe you should. I'll meet you outside."

He hung up and continued looking out the window. "He says she has been acting a little strange at home lately, too. He wants to hear more about what's been happening here. It would be good if you could tell him, Dallas, since you've been in the classroom when this has been going on. Do you think you could do that?"

"Sure."

"We're going to go out looking for her between here and her home and any other spots Mr. Lucas thinks she might go to. Just tell him everything, from the first time she acted differ-

ent from what you expected until today. And tell him everything, every detail you can remember."

"I'll try. Can I go with you?"

"You not only *may*, but you also must. We don't want to
waste any time."

"Should you call the police?"

"Not yet. If we can't find her, we'll have to."

We were standing on the curb out front when Mr. Lucas
pulled up in a late model luxury car. I knew him from church.
He was owner and president of a local company, about fifty
with gray hair, tall, and stocky. His suit coat was hung in the
back on a hook. He drove in a dress shirt with the sleeves rolled
up and his tie loosened.

I sat in the back, behind Mr. Garrison, so I could see Mr.
Lucas from the side. He looked worried.

"Dallas O'Neil here is one of your wife's top students. I've
asked him to tell you what's been happening in the classroom."

"I know him," Mr. Lucas said. "How ya doin', Dallas?"

I told the whole story as Mr. Lucas drove quickly toward
his home. He listened carefully, but he and Mr. Garrison were
also looking up and down every street for signs of Mrs. Lucas
or her car.

Mr. Lucas either shook his head or nodded knowingly at
everything I said. "It's been going on almost a year now," he
said.

"Really?" I said. "I only started noticing it last week."

"Well, it's been coming on gradually," he said. "It started
when I began having to get her up in the morning. I mean, this
woman is the original farm girl, up at the crack of dawn for her
devotions, getting ready, fixing breakfast, getting to school early. Didn't she usually get to school early, Mr. Garrison?"

"*Usually*? She has always been the first one here. Always
in her room and ready to go long before the students arrive. So,
you started having to get her up?"

"Yes, and she seemed disoriented. Didn't know where she was, who she was, who I was, what I wanted. Once she got some water in her face and coffee down her, she came around as usual, but I found that very strange after twenty-five years of living with someone who is usually wide awake from the word go."

"What did you make of it?" the principal asked.

"I'll tell you, the first time or two I merely thought it was curious. I thought maybe she had insomnia or had had bad dreams that robbed her of sleep. But when it continued, it scared me to death. I suggested we say something to the doctor, but she wouldn't hear of it."

"What did *she* think was causing it?"

"That's just it. For the first few weeks, she accused me of making it up. She didn't remember getting up, wouldn't really be conscious until she was at the breakfast table, then she would accuse me of having gotten her up when she was still asleep."

"Could she have been right?"

"No. She went to bed at the same time as usual, then I would let her sleep a half hour or even forty-five minutes longer than normal. Even with that, it took me fifteen minutes to gently talk her awake enough so that she would get up. If she was still asleep, she had no reason to be."

"Did all that bother her? Make her irritable?"

"It bothered her. She has never been hesitant to speak her mind, especially to me. But no, she would not become irritable. We never fought over it. We simply discussed it. She would not let me tell the doctor. Now I wish I had anyway."

He pulled into his own driveway, found the doors locked, the driveway and garage empty, and the oil spot on the ground dry. "She hasn't been here," he decided.

We drove to relatives' and friends' homes, where Mr. Lucas told them he needed to talk to his wife and wondered if they knew where she might have gone for lunch.

"You know she always eats at school," a friend told him. "She never goes out. What's the trouble?"

"Just looking for her," he said.

As we continued driving, trying to decide whether to involve the police, Mr. Lucas told Mr. Garrison that he didn't want to trouble or worry anyone until he had to.

"I understand," the principal said. "What other irregularities have you noticed in her?"

"Well, she used to tell me all about her school day, every evening. I got to know the kids as well as she did. In fact, Dallas, she's told me a lot about you and your sports team or something like that."

"The Baker Street Sports Club, yes, sir."

"That's right. She's told me all about that and about most of the students. The smart ones, the slow ones, the bright ones, the tough ones. They're all a challenge to her."

"And she quit talking about them all of a sudden, was that it?"

"No, she still talked about them, but she couldn't remember names as easily. That was bizarre. She has the original photographic memory. Can remember *anything*. Now I was having to remind her who was who. She would describe a kid, and I would suggest names. We laughed about it being old age and the memory being the first to go. It's not funny now."

11

The Discovery

The scariest part of Mr. Lucas's story was about the time when he was on his way out the door to work and the phone rang. "It was her," he said. "She was in a shopping center at that corner three blocks from the school."

"Wildwood?" Mr. Garrison said.

"Yeah, and she was crying. She said she got to the stoplight and went to turn on her blinker when she realized she was in the left lane. I said, 'What's wrong with that? You *want* to turn left there.' She says, 'I do?' I say, 'Of course, what's the problem?' 'Well,' she says, 'it just didn't seem right to go left. I thought sure I wanted to go right, but I couldn't do it from the left lane. I thought about going straight, but I knew that was wrong.'

"I said to her, 'So you called me to find out which way to turn?' I was sort of kidding because that was so absurd. I thought I would make a little light of it. She was not amused. I couldn't get her to quit crying. I asked her if she could find her way home, and she said of course she could. I told her to come on home and take the day off, that I would call you and arrange for a substitute.

"Well, that got her mad. She absolutely would not consider that. She said, 'Just tell me which way to turn there, and I can find the school.' I said, 'All right, you were in the left lane by instinct because you've been turning left at that corner for years. Go back out there and turn left and watch for the school on your left-hand side about three blocks up.'

"Then she asked me if I thought she was losing her mind. I said, 'No, you found a phone and remembered your own number, didn't you? You had a memory lapse. Nothing to worry about.' She hung up and went right to school. Later that day I asked her how her day went. She said fine, and she told me some stories, names and all. I didn't even remind her of her phone call that morning."

"Mr. Lucas," the principal said, "we have to go to the police. You know that, don't you?"

Mr. Lucas looked terribly sad. "Yes, sir, I do." He turned and drove to the station, where the police put out an all-points bulletin for Mrs. Lucas and her car, describing both. They took us to a small room with a few tables and some vending machines and told Mr. Lucas that "unless there was foul play—which we have no reason to believe—and if she has been gone only as long as you say, she can't have gone far. We'll find her soon enough. We'll keep you posted."

"Can't I go along and help out?"

"It'll be easier for us if you stay here. You'll be the first to know when we locate her. We'll call you, and then we'll bring her here. You know, she could have just run out on an errand."

"Yeah, I hope so."

We sat in silence for a few minutes.

"Dallas," the principal said, "I need to call the school so that if she comes back they can call us, and if she doesn't, your class will be covered." He gave me some change and told me to get myself and Mr. Lucas some lunch from the machines.

"I'm not real hungry," Mr. Lucas said.

90

"There's not much here anyway," I said, as Mr. Garrison left. "Is this how policemen eat?"

Mr. Lucas chuckled, then grew serious. "I should have taken her to the doctor months ago," he said.

"Yeah, I guess," I said. "But, like me, you didn't know what was wrong. And you said she didn't want you to tell the doctor. You can't *make* somebody get help, can you?"

"Oh, sure you can. I'm responsible for her. If I was having terrible chest pains and shortness of breath, I'd want her to force me to go to the doctor whether I wanted to or not. You know, she did that for me four years ago and saved my life."

"You had all that trouble, and you didn't want to go to the doctor?"

"Nope. I didn't want to find out I needed a bypass operation or was on the verge of a heart attack. I wanted to tough it out, beat it myself."

"I remember that. We prayed for you at church all the time. What exactly *was* wrong with you?"

"Just what I feared. I was on the verge, and I needed a bypass. Saved my life. I owe the same to her."

"What do you think her problem is?"

"I don't know. She seems awfully young for this Alzheimer's disease, but when I combine what you told me about how she is in class with what I know from home, that's what it sounds like. In fact, I think I'm going to call my doctor right now."

"What if she's out running an errand, like they said?"

"Nah, Dallas, she simply doesn't do that during the school day. She's always told me that she believes she belongs to that place from the time she gets there until the time she leaves. You know she even volunteers for lunchroom duty. In fact, I think she was supposed to be on lunch duty today. She may be at a store and come back with a story that she was running out for something, but I know different. I need to make that call."

He headed off down the hall to a pay phone, and there I sat, eating a stale sandwich and drinking a can of pop. I stood without thinking when a policeman came into the room.

"We've found her car," he said. "Out near the expressway. Where is her husband?"

"Down the hall on the phone," I said. "So is Mr. Garrison."

"I'll get them," the officer said.

I was still standing there a few minutes later when another officer brought a crying Mrs. Lucas into the room.

"M-Mrs. Lucas," I said. "Are you all right?"

"Dallas!" she said. "How good to see a friendly face! Yes, I'm all right now."

"Ma'am," the officer said, "you sit right here with this boy and don't leave, all right?"

She looked offended. "I have no intention of leaving."

"Yes, ma'am," he said, and he left.

"Where were you?" I asked.

She began to weep again. "I don't remember. They said they found my car near the frontage road and that I had wandered from house to house until I could find someone who would let me use their phone. Then I couldn't remember any numbers, and I had left my purse at school."

"How did they find you?"

"Oh, Dallas! I couldn't even remember my own name! The woman at the house asked me if I had a car, and I couldn't remember. I had walked several blocks. She said she could get my name if she knew my license number, but I couldn't even describe my car. She called the police to see if a middle-aged woman was missing, and they told her they had found my car and that I should be in the woman's neighborhood. She described me to them, and they told her to ask me if my name was Mrs. Lucas. Then it all came back to me. I feel so ashamed."

"There's nothing to be ashamed of, Mrs. Lucas. There's obviously something wrong, and you need help."

"Yes, but nobody wants to go crazy, Dallas. Have I been terrible in class?" I hated myself for hesitating, but when I did, she caught on right away. "Oh, I have, haven't I?"

"Well, I'd say you haven't been yourself."

Mr. Lucas burst through the door. "Honey," he said, and she stood to embrace him, sobbing. "The doctor is on his way. No arguments this time. We're getting to the bottom of this."

Sadly, Mr. Lucas's fears were accurate. His wife was diagnosed with Alzheimer's disease, even though she was younger than most who suffer from it. There is treatment for it, but no cure, and nothing that was done for Mrs. Lucas allowed her to come back to work.

On the last day of the school year, Mr. Garrison let our class, at Mr. Lucas's request, have a party at his home for our former teacher. Everyone pitched in a few dollars so we could buy her a plaque that honored her as the best teacher we had ever had.

It made her cry. She was doing pretty well that day, although sometimes it seemed she went into a little trance that nothing could penetrate. At other times, she was just like her old self. She knew what was wrong with her, she said. It frustrated her, puzzled her, challenged her, angered her, drew her closer to God. "I would study it until I beat it," she said, "if I could concentrate on it for even fifteen minutes at a time. My biggest fear is that I will embarrass myself or my family."

We hugged her and sang to her and wished her the best. Those of us who went to the same church her family did were able to see her occasionally when she was well enough to come. What little was known about the disease was obvious in Mrs. Lucas. She kept getting worse, forgetting more, remembering less, until she had to be in a wheelchair and hardly ever recognized anybody, even her own family.

Within a year she was put in the hospital for constant care. It was one of the saddest things I had ever seen. She wasn't given long to live, because eventually the disease affects the brain and the central nervous system, leaving a person unable to do anything for himself.

It was a tough lesson for me. I didn't like it, found it difficult to accept, and questioned God long and hard about it.

What did I learn? Only that I don't have to understand everything. Life isn't fair. Mrs. Lucas would be another one of those loved ones in my life who would only get better when she died.

I would never forget her though—the best teacher I ever had.

Moody Press, a ministry of the Moody Bible Institute, is designed for education, evangelization, and edification. If we may assist you in knowing more about Christ and the Christian life, please write us without obligation: Moody Press, c/o MLM, Chicago, Illinois 60610.